T0195977

Things Just Happen 24/7

24 Hours
a Day
7 Days
a Week

Written and Illustrated by
Suzie Caldwell

To order additional copies of this book, contact:
Xlibris
844-714-8691
www.Xlibris.com
Orders@Xlibris.com

ISBN: Softcover   978-1-6641-5252-6
        Hardcover   978-1-6641-5253-3
        EBook   978-1-6641-5251-9

Print information available on the last page

Rev. date: 04/15/2021

This book is dedicated to my daddy, Dr. Charles Keenan.
Thank you for being there for me 24/7.
RIP 5.21.1933 – 07.19.2015

I went kite flying on the beach with my parents and suddenly the wind picked up and my kite went crazy up high in the sky. My kite string went, "Snap!" And broke. I can always get another kite.

Things just happen 24/7 and that's okay.

Once Upon a time there was magical place All that went here saw only beautiful things. Everyone lived in a Castle and were never sad.

Ripped

My friend borrowed my favorite book and when she returned it, she had <u>Ripped</u> a page from my book. I can always get a new copy of my favorite book.

Things just happen 24/7 and that's okay.

I found a beautiful seashell along the beach and picked it up. A wave knocked me down and I dropped it in the ocean. I looked for it, but it was <u>Lost</u> forever. I can always find another seashell.

Things just happen 24/7 and that's okay.

My family and I were driving along in our car when suddenly we heard a, "<u>Pop!</u>" And then a hiss sound. My dad got out only to see what had happened. He told us it was our tire; but he had a spare. I can always count on my dad.

Things just happen 24/7 and that's okay.

I went to have my favorite Ice cream in the freezer, and it was <u>Gone</u>. Someone in my family had finished it and left the empty container in the freezer. I can always get new Ice cream. Things just happen 24/7 and that's okay.

We had left our house to run some errands and when we got home, there was a note on our front door. It read,

{We had come by to see you all, but you were not here.

Miss you XOXO Love, Grandpa and Grandma}.

I was <u>Disappointed</u> that they had come by our house and I did not get to see them. I can always plan another day, another time.

Things just happen 24/7 and that's okay.

I was at school having fun running around and then I fell hard on my knees. My Teacher cleaned them both up and put band-aids on my scrapes. I wanted to cry, but I was brave and just said, "<u>Ouch</u>!" I can always run around again.

Things just happen 24/7 and that's okay.

I was walking home from a friend's house and I saw something laying in the street. It was a bird; it did not move or blink. It laid there very still and was not in any pain. I said to myself, <u>Good-bye</u> to the bird. I can always see more birds.

Things just happen 24/7 and that's okay.

I had a <u>Horrible</u> stomachache and I had to go to the bathroom a lot! I could not go to my friend's house because my tummy hurt me. I can always go to my friend's house another time.

Things just happen 24/7 and that's okay.

My sister asked me if she could give me a <u>Hair-cut</u>. I told her yes but be careful because I love my long hair. She started to cut it to my shoulder! I looked in the mirror, it was way too short. She ended up cutting the other side, so it was the same and leaving the back long. I can always grow my hair again. Things just happen 24/7 and that's okay.

I was painting a beautiful water coloring picture and I accidentally smeared it with my hand. This made me feel <u>Frustrated</u>. I can always paint another picture.

Things just happen 24/7 and that's okay.

A popular boy in my classroom was having a birthday party and he was passing out invitations for his party. Then suddenly, I felt a tap on my shoulder, it was his twin sister, <u>Yay!</u> She had invited me to the party. I can always go to birthday parties when I am invited.

Things just happen 24/7 and that's okay.

My big brother always sneezed when he got around our new pet dog, named Max. My brother's nose and eyes were always itchy and watery. My Mom took him to the Doctor's, and it turned out he was <u>Allergic</u> to dog's. We ended up giving Max to our Uncle. I can always visit Max.

Things just happen 24/7 and that's okay.

Our vegetable garden grows delicious tomatoes. I went outside to pick a big, ripe tomato and by the time I got to the kitchen, it had a green horned worm crawling out of it, <u>Yuck</u>! I can always get another tomato.

Things just happen 24/7 and that's okay.

It was late in the evening and I got hungry. I wanted a snack, so I decided to have milk and cookies. I went to the cookie jar and set out two chocolate chip cookies and put them on my plate. Then I got a glass out of the cupboard and when I went to get the milk from the refrigerator, there was <u>No Milk?</u> I can always get more milk.

Things just happen 24/7 and that's okay.

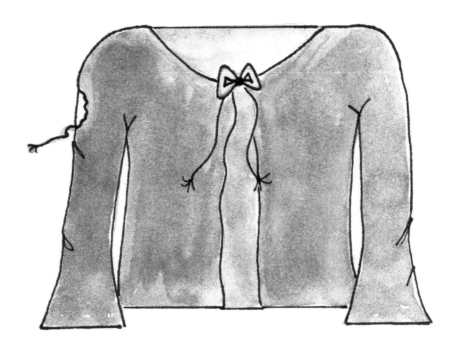

It was my friend's birthday and I wanted to dress-up for the occasion. I had the perfect dress, shoes, and sweater. I looked in the mirror and saw a hole in my sweater and I shouted, "<u>Yikes</u>!" Thank goodness I tried on my sweater before I left. I put on a different sweater and it looked pretty. I can always change my clothes.

Things just happen 24/7 and that's okay.

I took my bracelet off, so I could jump rope with my friends and laid it carefully down. My friends and I had fun Jump roping together. When we were finished, I went inside my house. I looked down at my wrist and I was not aware that I had taken it off. I went back outside and saw a sparkle and knew my bracelet was still there! I felt <u>Joy</u> all over me. I can always feel good when I find, what I have lost.

Things just happen 24/7 and that's okay.

My friend has cancer, and he was losing his hair. I bought him a cool, new baseball cap for him to wear. When I arrived at the hospital with it, I saw a nice boy talking to him and he was saying your hair will grow back. This gave me <u>Hope</u> because I care for him. I can always have wonderful feelings for him.

Things just happen 24/7 and that's okay.

I woke-up with a funny looking rash and it was so itchy. I told my Mom about it and showed her. She said, "You will need to see a <u>Doctor</u> for that rash, his name is Dr. Keenan." It turned out to be chicken pox and I cannot go to school until it scabs over, because I am still contagious. I can always know this itchy rash will go away.

Things just happen 24/7 and that's okay.

I was having an exciting time playing outside in the sunshine when suddenly, it started to <u>Rain</u>! I ran inside and dried myself off. I can always know the sunshine will come again.

Things just happen 24/7 and that's okay.

One day I decided to take my neighbor's dog for a walk while riding my bike. I held the leash tight in my hand and tried hopping on the seat, but he pulled me down to the ground before I could sit. A boy was skateboarding down the street and laughed when he saw what had happened. I said to the boy, "That's <u>Not nice!</u> I am hurt." I took the dog back to the neighbor's and went inside my house to get a band-aid for my scraped shoulder.

I can always know riding my bike and walking a dog is not a clever idea, for now.

Things just happen 24/7 and that's okay.

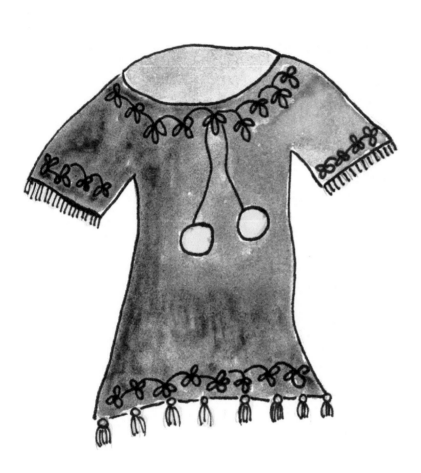

I made good grades in school during the year, so my parents took me shopping. I got a few things, but my favorite was a <u>Pretty</u> new top. I loved it and wore it to school one day. I went to P. E. and put it in my gym locker, but someone took it. I can always get a new top that is similar.

Things just happen 24/7 and that's okay.

Cozy

My sister and I decided to camp in our backyard one night. We had our big brother's set-up our tent for us. We brought blankets, pillows, popcorn, and flashlights. That made our tent real <u>Cozy</u> and fun for the night. My sister got scared though and she decided to go back in the house and sleep. I did not want to be by myself, so I went in too. I can always plan another night in our tent.

Things just happen 24/7 and that's okay.

I went outside to play on my swing that hung on a big tree branch from our giant tree. When I looked it was not there, it had been cut down. I was so <u>Surprised</u> that it was gone, but it was not safe because it had suffered tree rot. I can always figure out a new spot for my tree swing.

Things just happen 24/7 and that's okay.

My Dad and Mom had us sit on the couch to tell us something. We had no idea what it was about. Then my Mom kindly said to us, "I'm going to have a baby." We were so Excited; it was great news. I can always feel safe and fine when my parents have news for us; either bad or good.

Things just happen 24/7 and that's okay.

The End

That's okay

Printed in the United States
by Baker & Taylor Publisher Services